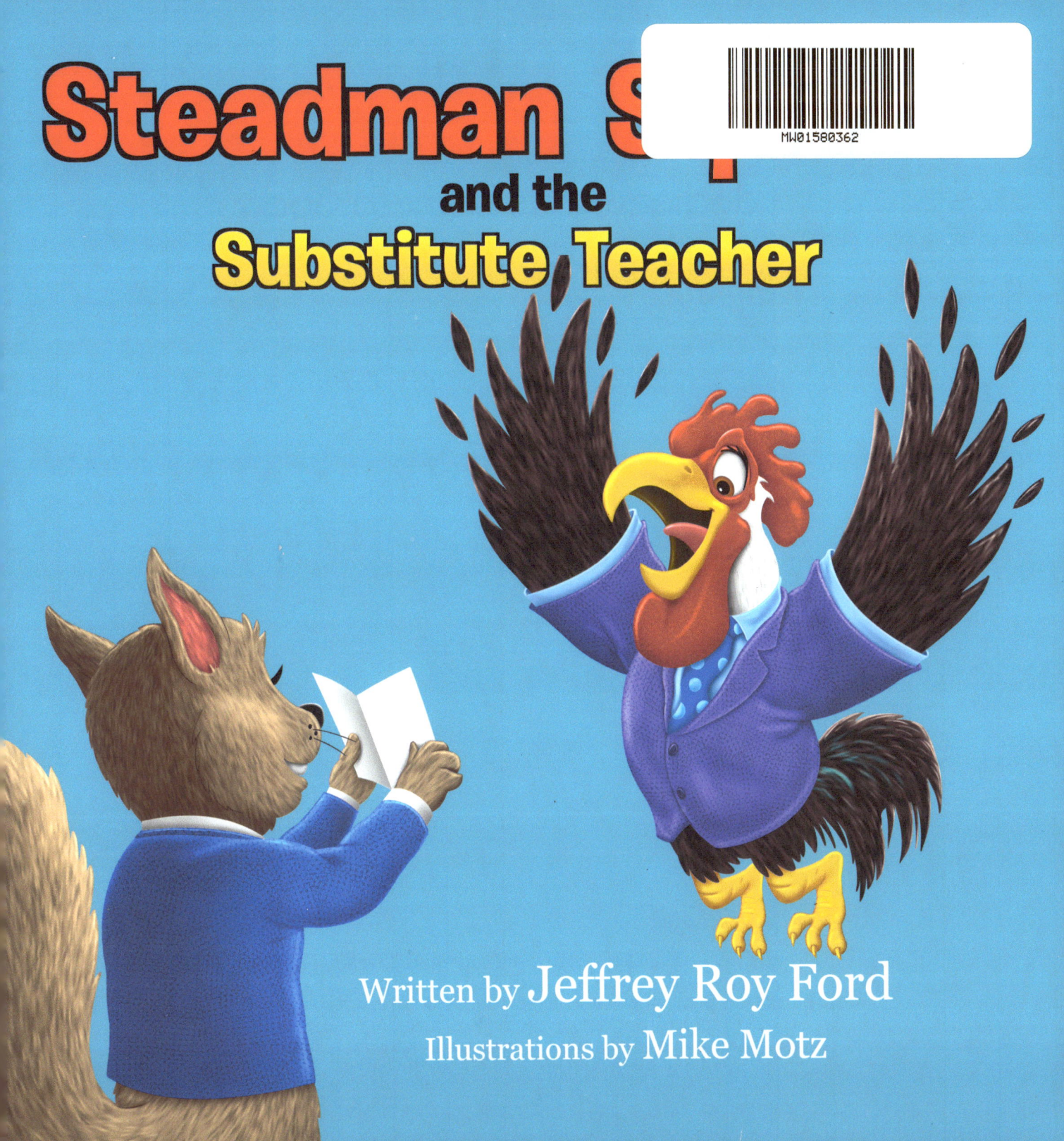

I dedicate this book to God,
my family, and my friends.

Steadman Squirrel and the Substitute Teacher
© 2023 Jeffrey Roy Ford. All Rights reserved.
No part of this publication may be reproduced or transmitted in any form
or by any means, electronic, mechanical, including photocopy,
recording, or any information storage and retrieval system,
without permission in writing from the author.

Steadman Squirrel
and the Substitute Teacher

Written by Jeffrey Roy Ford

Illustrations by Mike Motz

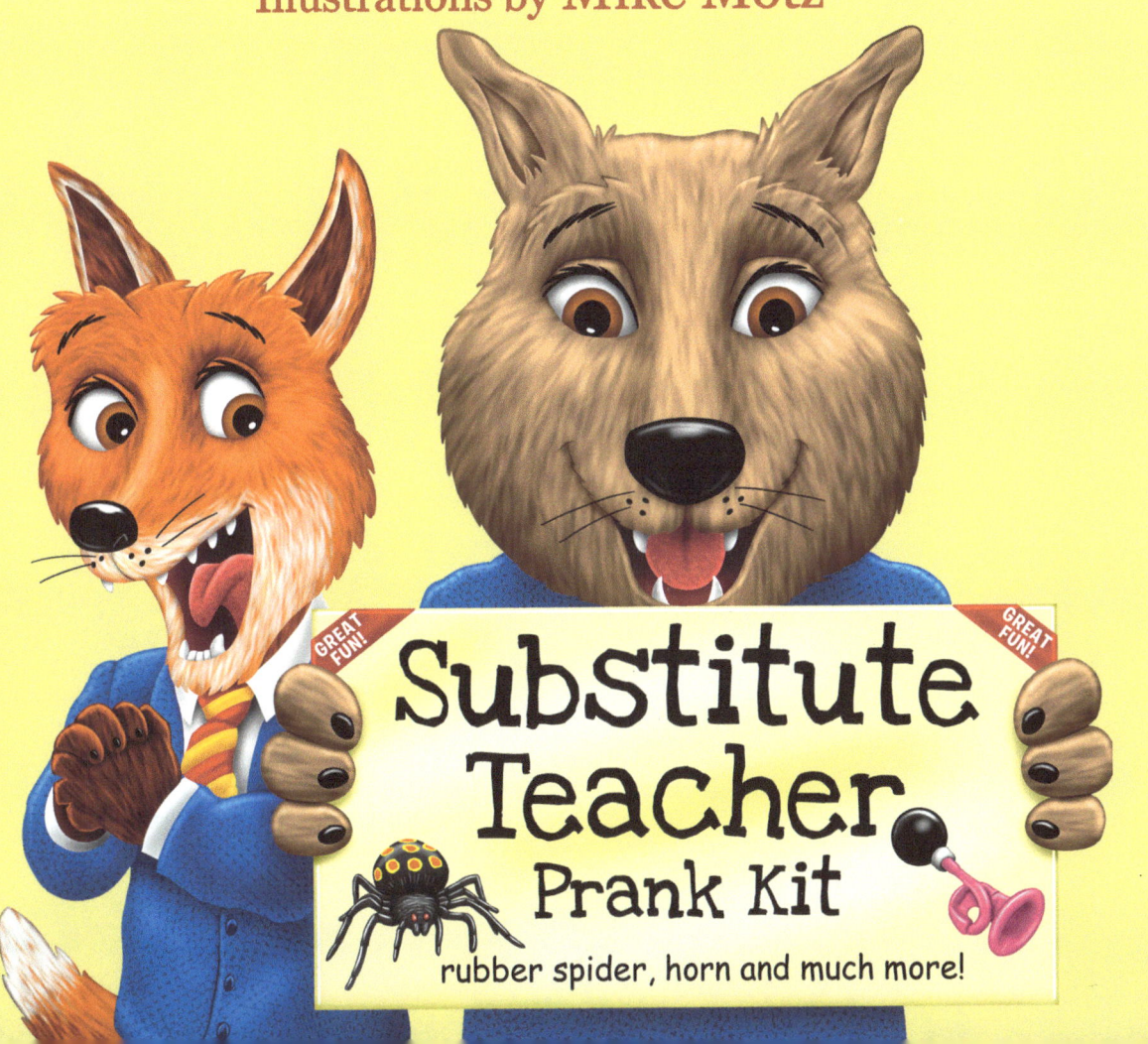

Steadman Squirrel is in class at Banana Nut Creek Elementary School. He is doing a math assignment with his best friends, Rema Rabbit and Rashawn Racoon.

Their teacher, Mr. Dorian Dog, taps the bell on his desk. "Class, I have an announcement. I am leaving early today. This afternoon you will have a substitute teacher, and his name is Mr. Rooster. It's his first-day teaching, so be nice to him."

Mr. Rooster walks into the classroom. He starts to sweat, and his legs tremble as the students stare at him. "Um, um, hello, class. My name is Mr. Rufus Rooster."

Suddenly, a cell phone rings in the class, scaring Mr. Rooster. He jumps up and down as feathers fly off him. "Eek! Eek! Doodle-do! Doodle-do!"

Steadman and the other students put their hands over their mouths as they try not to laugh.

Steadman eats in the cafeteria with Rema and Rashawn.

"We have a sub today. The class is going to be so loud and mean," Rema mentions.

"My mom always taught me to respect all my teachers," Rashawn says.

Steadman barely hears what his friends are saying because he's watching Wally Wolf and Fernando Fox at the next table. "They are the coolest kids in school. I wish I could be friends with them," Steadman says.

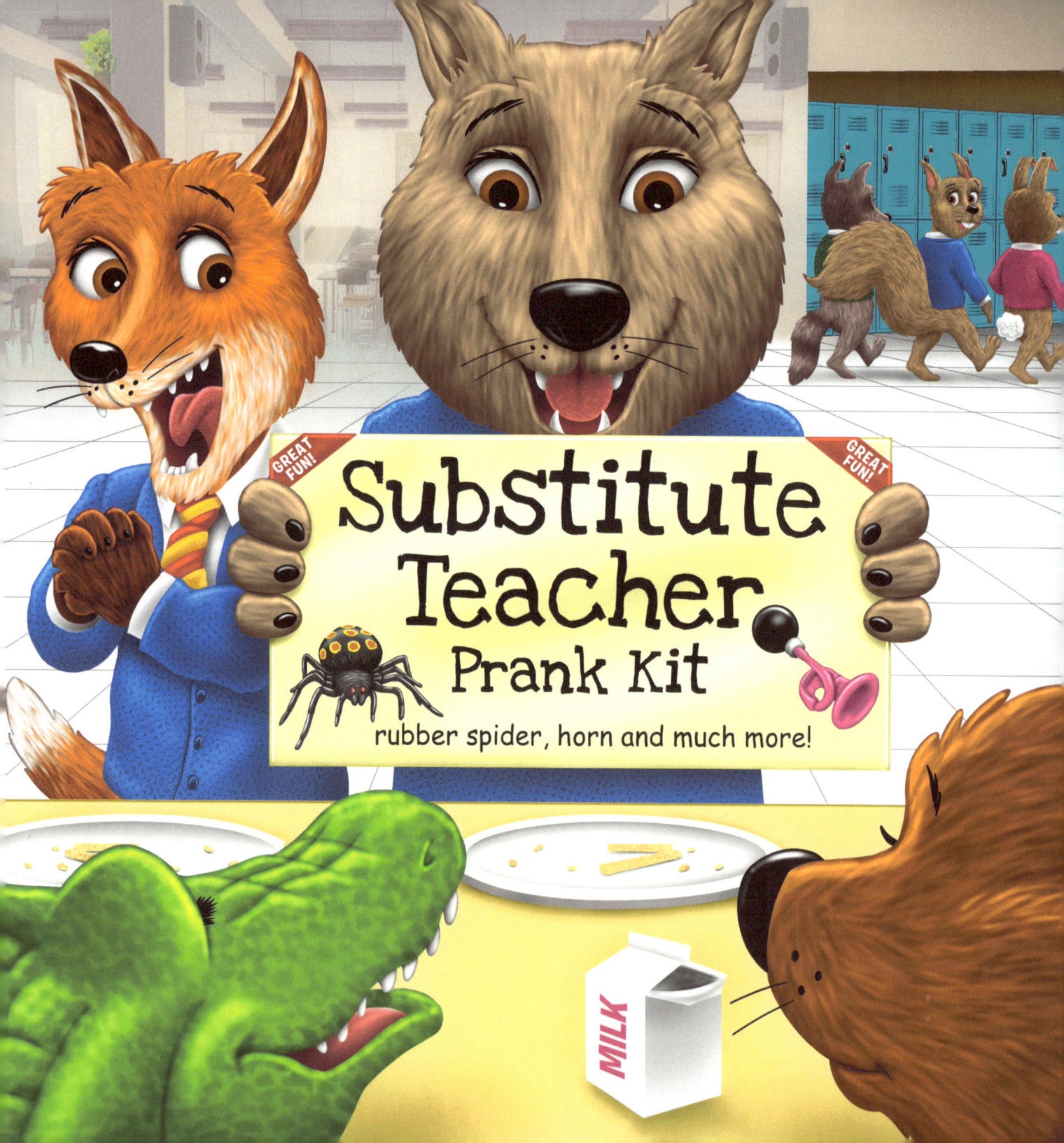

Wally pulls out his substitute teacher's prank kit to show the other students.

Fernando rubs his furry hands together. "Today is going to be so fun!"

The students return to class.

Mr. Rooster shakes as he writes his name on the chalkboard. He notices the students are in different seats than they were in the morning. "Um, um, everyone, please sit in your assigned seats," Mr. Rooster begs.

"We are in our assigned seats," Fernando chuckles.

"Way to lie to the sub," Wally says.

Wally sneaks to the front of the class and puts a rubber spider on the teacher's desk.

Mr. Rooster sees it and jumps. "Eek! Eek! Doodle-do! Doodle-do!"

The class laughs as his feathers float in the air.

Steadman, Rashawn, and Rema remain in their seats as their classmates begin talking loudly.

Mr. Rooster tries his best to teach the class their math lesson, but no one is listening to him.

Wally and Fernando go over to Steadman.

"Hey, Steadman, you should blow this horn in Mr. Rooster's ear," Wally says.

"If you do, you can come to my birthday party," Fernando mentions.

"Wow! That's going to be the biggest party of the year," Steadman replies.

Steadman takes the horn and tiptoes to the front of the class.

"Don't do it," Rashawn says.

"This is mean. You are going to get in trouble," Rema states.

Steadman gets behind a sad Mr. Rooster. He sees a picture of him and his family on the teacher's desk. "I can't do this."

Steadman returns to his seat.

"You're a bigger chicken than the sub, Steadman," Wally says.

Wally and Fernando take the horn and go toward Mr. Rooster.

Principal Pandra Pig hears the commotion from the hallway and enters the classroom. "Wally and Fernando! My office—now!"

Principal Pig lectures the class. "Everyone, get in your assigned seats. It is rude to be disrespectful to Mr. Rooster. He came out of his way to be your teacher. No more talking for the rest of the day!"

Steadman sits quietly in his seat and frowns. "I wish my classmates hadn't behaved so badly."

He takes out his crayons and begins to draw. At the end of the class, Steadman gives Mr. Rooster a card that he made. "Thank you for being my teacher."

A big smile comes across Mr. Rooster's face, and he happily flaps his wings. "Doodle-do! Doodle-do! You just made my day."

Steadman leaves the class. "I will always respect my teacher and be kind to others."

The End

Meet
Jeffrey Roy Ford

Jeffrey Roy Ford is an animal lover and former substitute teacher. He has dedicated his life to making a difference by using his love for animals to create fun stories that teach children important life lessons.

CPSIA information can be obtained
at www.ICGtesting.com
Printed in the USA
JSHW072100080623
42959JS00001B/1